by
Carolyn Crimi

Tessa's Tip-Tapping Toes

illustrated by
Marsha Gray
Carrington

SCHOLASTIC INC.
New York   Toronto   London   Auckland   Sydney
Mexico City   New Delhi   Hong Kong   Buenos Aires

ISBN 0-439-53105-5

Text copyright © 2002 by Carolyn Crimi.
Illustrations copyright © 2002 by Marsha Gray Carrington.
All rights reserved. Published by Scholastic Inc.
SCHOLASTIC and associated logos are trademarks
and/or registered trademarks of Scholastic Inc.

12 11 10 9 8 7 6 5 4 3 2 1   3 4 5 6 7 8/0

Printed in the U.S.A.   14

Book design by Nancy Goldenberg
The text of this book is set in 14 point Hiroshige Medium.
The illustrations are acrylic.

For my nieces and nephews—Katelyn, Justin, Dorothy, Robert, Max, Olivia, and Jack.

With special thanks to Cynthia Leitich Smith, who helped Tessa dance.—C.C.

For my mom,
a constant source of creative inspiration,
and my dad, an endless source of
kid inspiration.
I love you. —M.G.C.

*T*essa had swinging arms, skipping feet,
and tip-tapping toes. She was built to dance.

Most mice scurried along
floorboards and ledges,
trying not to be seen.
Not Tessa.

She boogied, she bopped,

she shimmied, she hopped,

she flounced and she bounced, but she never scurried.

"Tessa! Stop twirling so!" her mother would scold.

Tessa would try to stop with every ounce of her be-boppin', hip-hoppin' heart. But when her toes weren't tip-tapping, they felt all wrong.

At night Tessa and her family raided Mrs. Timboni's kitchen, hunting for crumbs. But instead of hurrying and scurrying, Tessa juggled jelly beans and sashayed with saltshakers. She loved to tap-dance across the teapot, wearing her bottle-cap slippers.

Clickity-clack-clack, Tessa danced.

Then one day Mrs. Timboni got a cat.
His name was Oscar, and his head was
filled with songs.

Most cats liked dozing on windowsills
or curling up on fresh piles of laundry.

Not Oscar. He crooned on the kitchen counters,

sang in the sinks,

and trilled on the dining room table.

"Oscar! Stop all that racket!" cried Mrs. Timboni.
"What will the neighbors think!"

Oscar tried stopping
with every ounce of his
singsongy humdinger of
a heart. But when his
tongue wasn't trilling,
he felt all wrong.

As soon as Tessa's mother heard Oscar's crooning, she worried that the new cat would catch her dancing daughter.

"You must be more careful!" she told Tessa. "No more bounding! No leaping! No spinning! From now on you will scamper and scurry like a proper mouse!"

So Tessa hurried and scurried. She skittered and scampered. She stayed low to the ground and didn't make a sound.

But it was hard, so hard. When she heard Oscar's songs, Tessa bit her tail to keep herself from dancing.

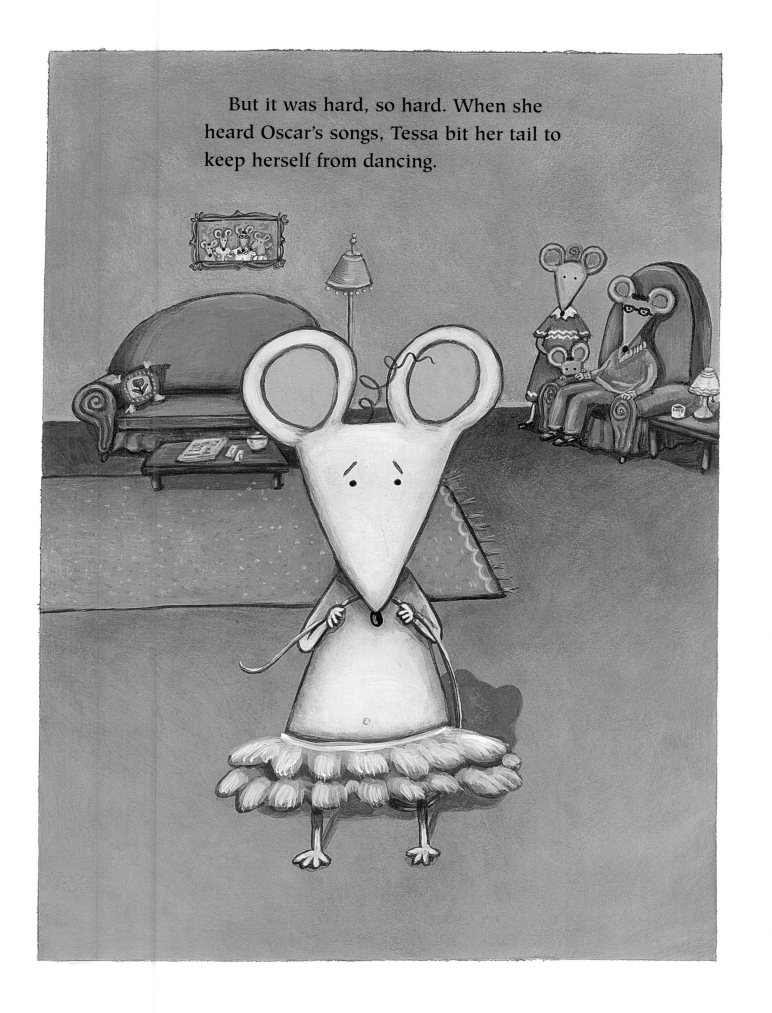

Within a week the neighbors complained about Oscar. Mrs. Timboni worried that they would ask her to get rid of her chorusing kitty.

"You must be more careful!" she told Oscar. "No more singing! No crooning or caterwauling! From now on you will nap and chase mice like a proper cat!"

So Oscar napped until noon and dozed right through dinner. At night he chased the hurrying, scurrying mice back into their holes.

But it was hard, so hard. When he heard the skitter-scamper of little mice feet, Oscar bit his tongue to keep himself from singing.

Then spring came.

Dozens of daffodils danced in the yard, and green leaves rustled in the breeze.

Tessa watched the daffodils sway. She longed to dance, but she remembered her mother's warning and kept still.

Oscar listened to the leaves swish. He longed to sing, but he remembered Mrs. Timboni's warning and kept silent.

Until one night when Oscar was awakened by the *ting, ting, ting* of rain on the roof.

Oscar's tongue twitched. His throat throbbed. His teeth chattered and his lips quivered. Before he knew it, a song sprang out of his mouth.

"*Doo-Whappa-Whappa Doo-Whappa-Whappa!*" he sang. "*Doo-Lang-Doo Lang-Doo-Lang . . .*"

Doo-Whappa-Whappa

CAT NAP

Doo-Whappa-Whappa! Doo-Lang-Doo Lang-Doolang

That same sliver of song wove its way into Tessa's dreams. Her tail curled. Her fingers snapped. Her head be-bobbed and her toes tip-tapped. Without opening her eyes, she waltzed toward the dancing sounds.

Diddle

The rain poured down harder and harder. Oscar sang louder and louder. *"Diddle-diddle dee-dee! Diddle dee-dee! Doodle wop-wop! Doodle wop-wop!"*

Tessa frolicked and frisked in time to the song.
She danced round and round until she lost her balance
and bumped into Oscar's food bowl with a clatter.

Suddenly Tessa woke up.

Oscar stopped singing. He spun toward the noise.

Cat and mouse stood staring at each other. All was quiet except for the rain on the roof.

Only one thing came to Tessa's mind. Before
Oscar could twitch a whisker, Tessa tip-tapped her
toes in time to the rain.
Oscar's mouth dropped open.
Tessa wiggled her middle to a clap of thunder.
Oscar shook his head and blinked.

Tessa burst into an all-out rock-'n'-roll, boogie-woogie, hip-hop, two-step combo.

Oscar watched, eyes wide. Finally he cleared his throat and belted out a rowdy, riotous tune just right for dancing feet.

Tessa moved to the groove. *Up, down, round and round! Jump, shout, kick it out! Swing, swoosh, shake it loose!* She felt so good she couldn't stop if she tried.

Tessa's mother crept carefully out of her hole. "Tessa, stop!" she whispered.

But Tessa couldn't hear her. She kept dancing to Oscar's song.

Then Mrs. Timboni rushed down to the kitchen in her bathrobe. "Oscar, stop!" she pleaded.

But Oscar couldn't hear her. He kept singing to Tessa's dancing.

Before long, Tessa's mother's tail twitched. She tapped her tiny toes.

Then Mrs. Timboni's throat itched. She hummed a little tune.

Soon everyone was dancing and singing along with Oscar's song.

"Doo-wang-doodle bang-doodle-doodle-doo!"

By the time the neighbors called to complain, no one
could even hear the phone ring.

And they danced—*hippy hop-hop*—and they sang—
doodle wop-wop—all night long.